THE ABOMINABLE SNOWMAN MYSTERY

By Shannon Penney ▪ Illustrated by Duendes del Sur
Hello Reader — Level 1

SCHOLASTIC INC.

New York   Toronto   London   Auckland   Sydney
Mexico City   New Delhi   Hong Kong   Buenos Aires

No part of this work may be reproduced, or stored in a retrieval system, or transmitted in any form or by any means, electronic, mechanical, photocopying, recording, or otherwise, without written permission of the publisher. For information regarding permission, write to Scholastic Inc., Attention: Permissions Department, 557 Broadway, New York, NY 10012.

ISBN 0-439-78549-9

12   11   10   9   8   10 11 12 13 14/0

Printed in the U.S.A.   40
First printing, November 2005

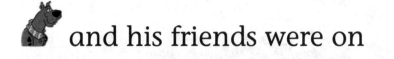 and his friends were on

vacation in the 🏔. They were

staying in a .

🐕 , 🧑, and the rest of the gang

were ready to ski and have fun in

the ❄️.

There were lots of fun activities!

Everyone bundled up. They each

wore a 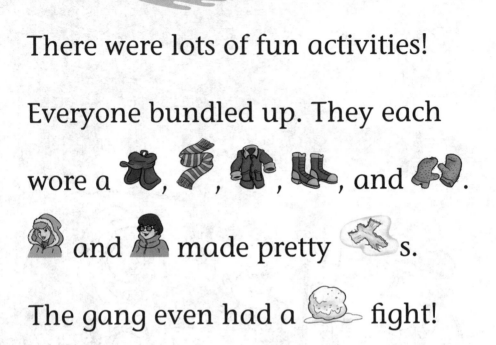, , , , and .

and made pretty s.

The gang even had a fight!

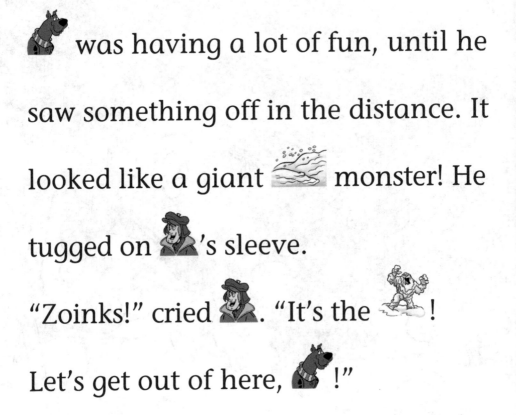 was having a lot of fun, until he saw something off in the distance. It looked like a giant monster! He tugged on 's sleeve.

"Zoinks!" cried . "It's the !

Let's get out of here, !"

 and ran into the . Their friends didn't know they were running from the .

"Good idea! Let's all go inside to warm up," said.

Everyone left their outside the back of the .

"Once we're warm and dry again, we can go skiing!" said .

Inside the 🏠, the gang sat on the

🛋. They drank hot chocolate and

🍬 from big ☕.

🐕 and 🧑 played games in front of

the 🔥. They had so much fun, they

forgot about the ⛄.

After a while, everyone was toasty

and ready to ski!

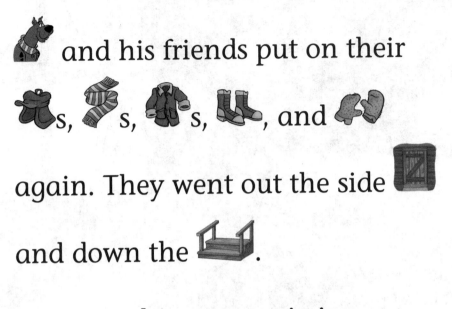 and his friends put on their s, s, s, , and again. They went out the side and down the . But something was missing. Their had disappeared!

"Oh, no!" said 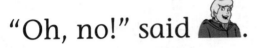.

"We can't go skiing without our 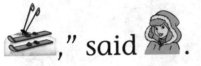," said 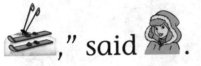.

"Zoinks!" cried 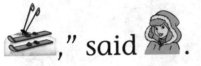, pointing into the distance. "It's the 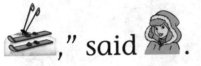! I'll bet he took our 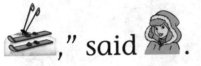, and now he's after us!"

"Let's look around," 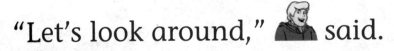 said.

"Maybe someone just moved our ."

 walked through the deep  around the . He didn't see the  anywhere.

When  came back,  and  were huddled together, shivering.

But they were not cold. They were afraid of the !

"Maybe someone moved our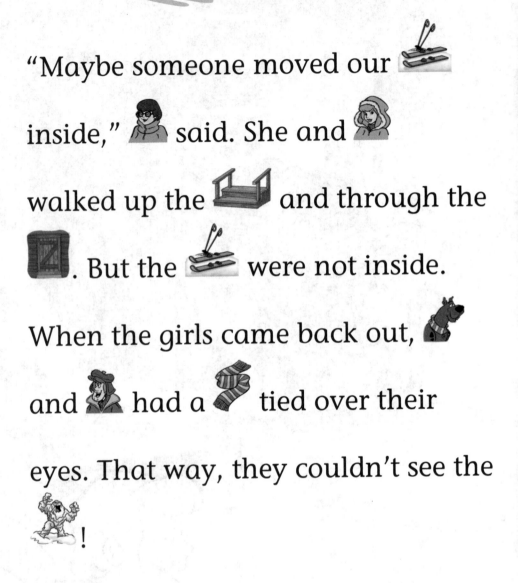

inside," 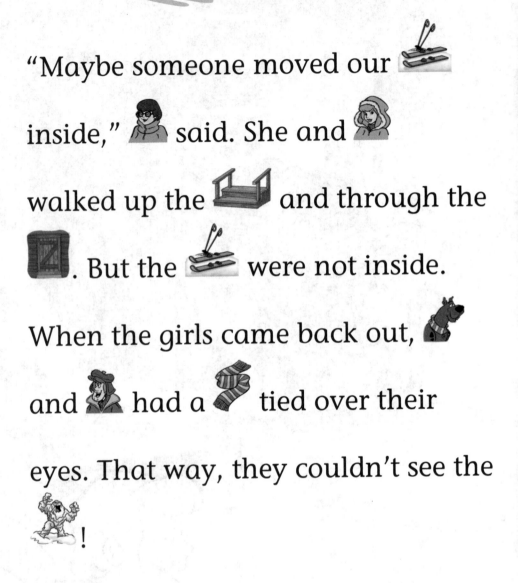 said. She and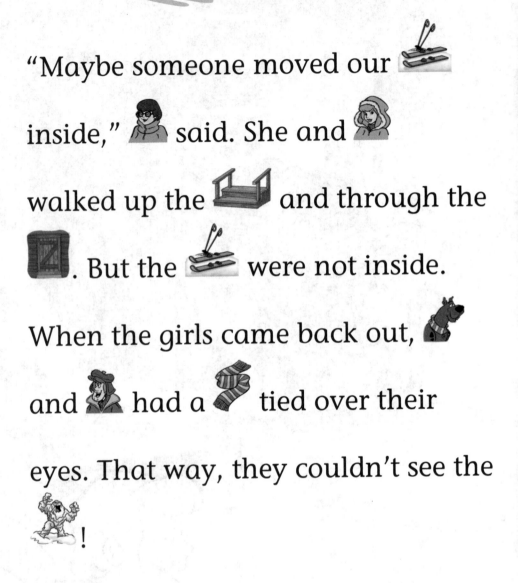

walked up the 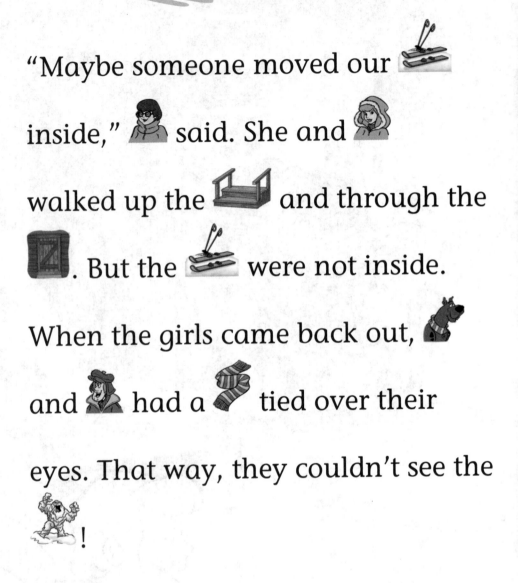 and through the

. But the were not inside.

When the girls came back out,

and had a tied over their

eyes. That way, they couldn't see the

!

"The 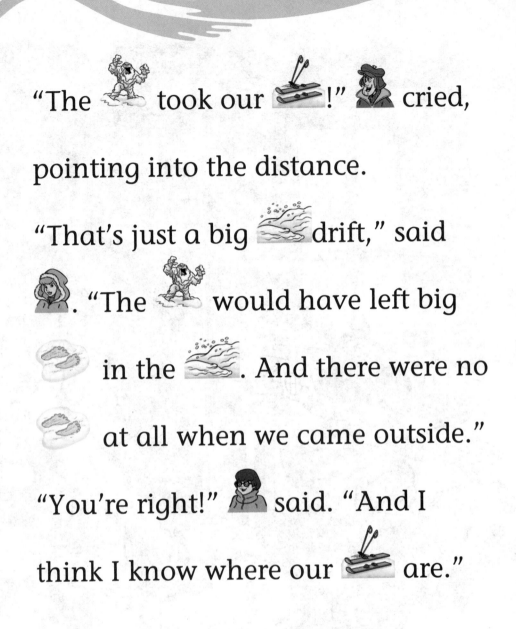 took our !" cried,

pointing into the distance.

"That's just a big drift," said

. "The would have left big

in the . And there were no

at all when we came outside."

"You're right!" said. "And I

think I know where our are."

 dug down in the ☁️ and pulled up a pair of 🎿.

"It must have snowed while we were inside," she said. "The ☁️ covered up our 🎿, and our ✈️s from before!"

🐕 pulled his 🎿 from under the ☁️. The 👹 didn't take them after all!

"Rooby-dooby-do!" 🐕 cheered.

Did you spot all the picture clues in this Scooby-Doo mystery?

Each picture clue is on a flash card. Ask a grown-up to cut out the flash cards. Then try reading the words on the back of the cards. The pictures will be your clue.

Reading is fun with Scooby-Doo!

Shaggy

Scooby

Daphne

Fred

lodge

Velma

snow

mountains

scarf

hat

boots

coat

snow angel | mittens

abominable
snowman | snowball

couch | skis

mugs

marshmallows

door

fire

footprints

stairs